DEC 19

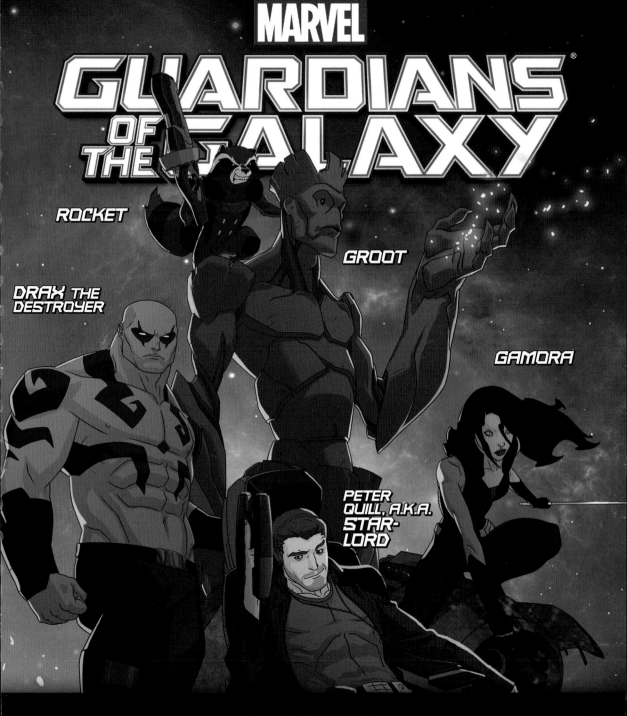

MARVEL
GUARDIANS OF THE GALAXY ®

ROCKET

GROOT

DRAX THE DESTROYER

GAMORA

PETER QUILL, A.K.A. STAR-LORD

PREVIOUSLY:

The Guardians came into possession of a mysterious Spartaxan cube that holds a map to an object of immense power called the Cosmic Seed. Half Spartaxan, Star-Lord is the only one able to access the map. Now the Guardians must find the Seed before Thanos does.

Volume 7: The Backstabbers
BASED ON THE DISNEY XD ANIMATED TV SERIES

Written by ANDREW R. ROBINSON   Directed by JAMES YANG
Animation Art Produced by MARVEL ANIMATION STUDIOS   Adapted by JOE CARAMAGNA

Special Thanks to
HANNAH MACDONALD & PRODUCT FACTORY and ANTHONY GAMBINO

MARK BASSO editor
AXEL ALONSO editor in chief
DAN BUCKLEY publisher

MARK PANICCIA senior editor
JOE QUESADA chief creative officer
ALAN FINE executive producer

ABDOBOOKS.COM

Reinforced library bound edition published in 2020 by Spotlight,
a division of ABDO, PO Box 398166, Minneapolis, Minnesota 55439.
Spotlight produces high-quality reinforced library bound editions for
schools and libraries. Published by agreement with Marvel Characters, Inc.

Printed in the United States of America, North Mankato, Minnesota.
042019
092019

THIS BOOK CONTAINS
RECYCLED MATERIALS

marvelkids.com
© 2020 MARVEL

Library of Congress Control Number: 2018965973

Publisher's Cataloging-in-Publication Data

Names: Caramagna, Joe; Robinson, Andrew R., authors. | Marvel Animation
    Studios, illustrator.
Title: The backstabbers / by Joe Caramagna ; Andrew R. Robinson; illustrated by
    Marvel Animation Studios.
Description: Minneapolis, Minnesota : Spotlight, 2020. | Series: Guardians of the
    Galaxy set 3 ; volume 7
Summary: Gamora gets mixed-up in a dangerous plan to pit Korath the Pursuer
    and Nebula against one another as they compete to become Thanos' new
    general.
Identifiers: ISBN 9781532143588 (lib. bdg.)
Subjects: LCSH: Guardians of the Galaxy (Fictitious characters)--Juvenile fiction. |
    Superheroes--Juvenile fiction. | Generals--Juvenile fiction. | Graphic novels--
    Juvenile fiction. | Gamora (Fictitious character)--Juvenile fiction. | Space--
    Juvenile fiction. | Comic books, strips, etc--Juvenile fiction.
Classification: DDC 741.5--dc23

Spotlight

A Division of ABDO
abdobooks.com

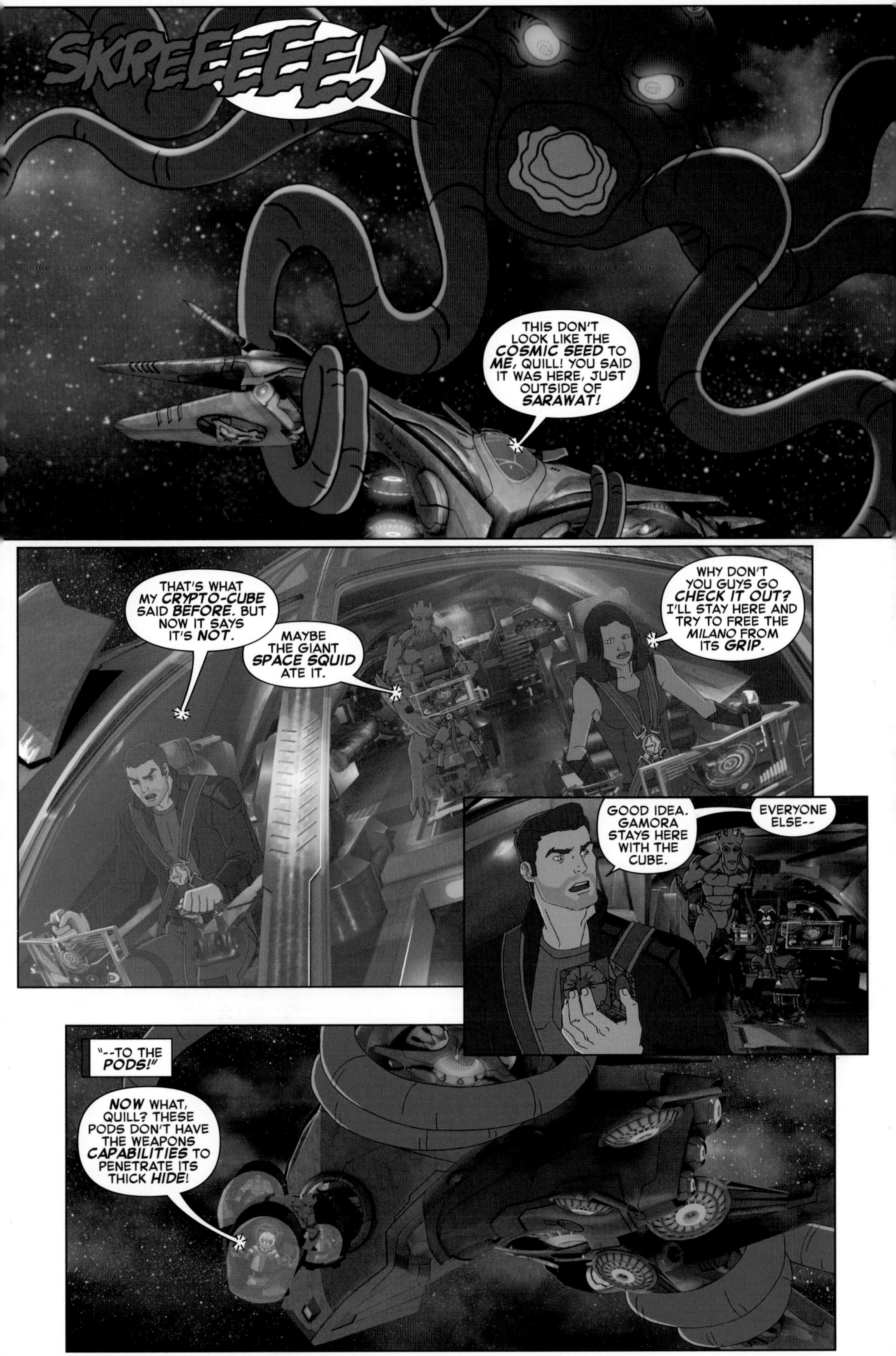
SKREEEEEE!
THIS DON'T LOOK LIKE THE COSMIC SEED TO ME, QUILL! YOU SAID IT WAS HERE, JUST OUTSIDE OF SARAWAT!
THAT'S WHAT MY CRYPTO-CUBE SAID BEFORE. BUT NOW IT SAYS IT'S NOT.
MAYBE THE GIANT SPACE SQUID ATE IT.
WHY DON'T YOU GUYS GO CHECK IT OUT? I'LL STAY HERE AND TRY TO FREE THE MILANO FROM ITS GRIP.
GOOD IDEA. GAMORA STAYS HERE WITH THE CUBE.
EVERYONE ELSE--
"--TO THE PODS!"
NOW WHAT, QUILL? THESE PODS DON'T HAVE THE WEAPONS CAPABILITIES TO PENETRATE ITS THICK HIDE!

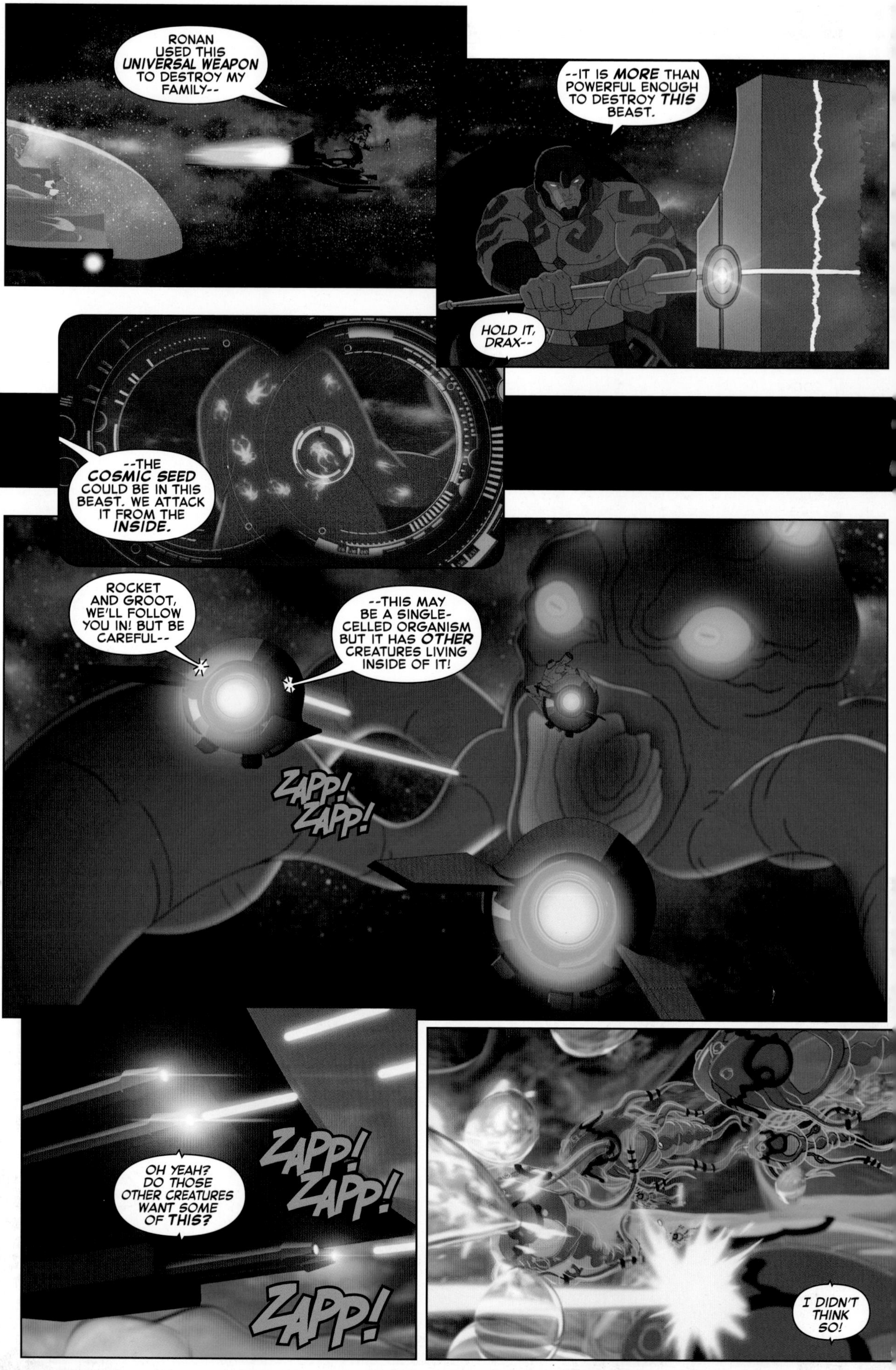
RONAN USED THIS UNIVERSAL WEAPON TO DESTROY MY FAMILY--
--IT IS MORE THAN POWERFUL ENOUGH TO DESTROY THIS BEAST.
HOLD IT, DRAX--
--THE COSMIC SEED COULD BE IN THIS BEAST. WE ATTACK IT FROM THE INSIDE.
ROCKET AND GROOT, WE'LL FOLLOW YOU IN! BUT BE CAREFUL--
--THIS MAY BE A SINGLE-CELLED ORGANISM BUT IT HAS OTHER CREATURES LIVING INSIDE OF IT!
ZAPP! ZAPP!
OH YEAH? DO THOSE OTHER CREATURES WANT SOME OF THIS?
ZAPP! ZAPP!
ZAPP!
I DIDN'T THINK SO!

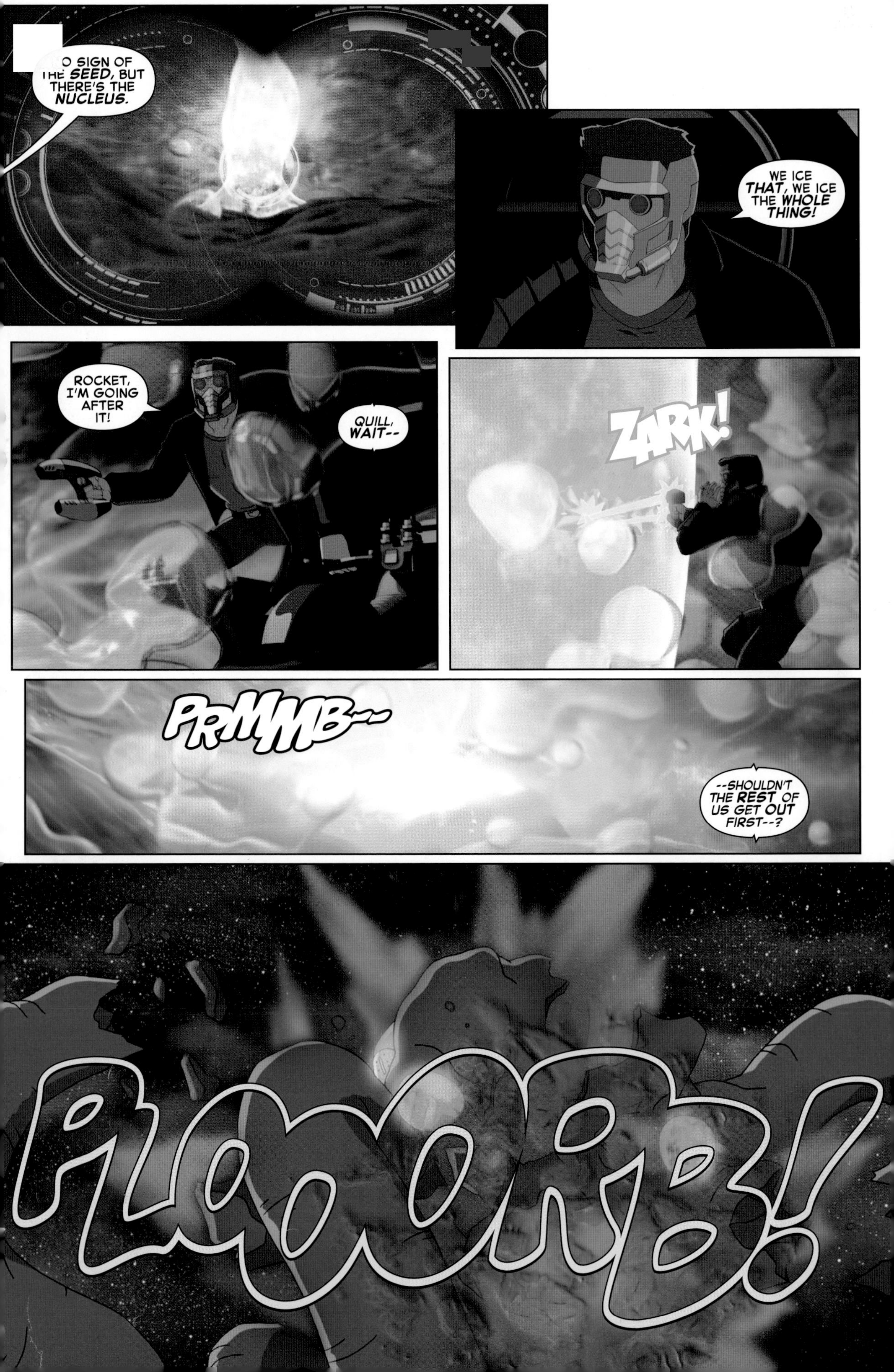
O SIGN OF THE SEED, BUT THERE'S THE NUCLEUS.
WE ICE THAT, WE ICE THE WHOLE THING!
ROCKET, I'M GOING AFTER IT!
QUILL, WAIT--
ZARK!
PRMMMB--
--SHOULDN'T THE REST OF US GET OUT FIRST--?

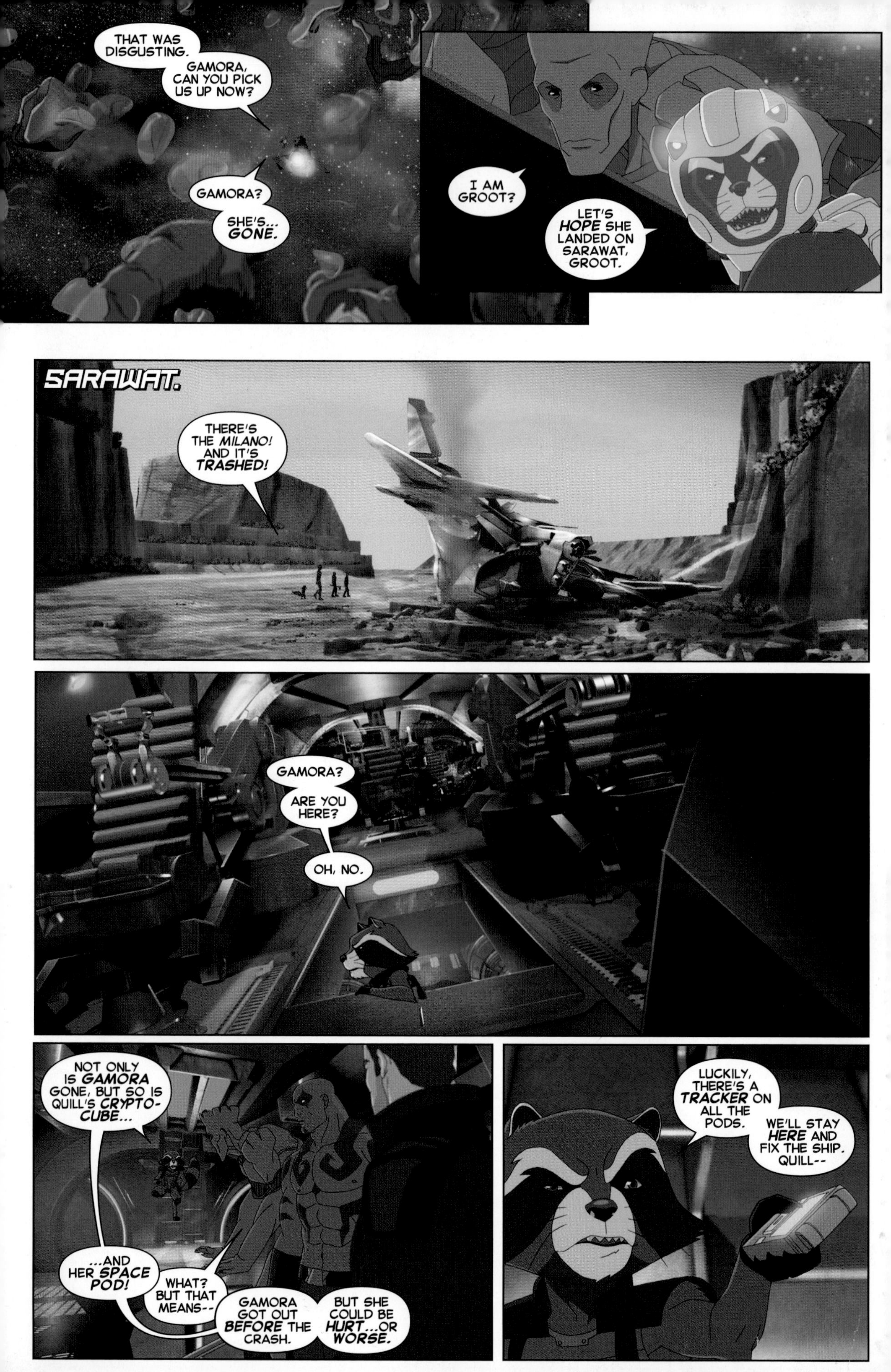
THAT WAS DISGUSTING.
GAMORA, CAN YOU PICK US UP NOW?
GAMORA?
SHE'S... GONE.
I AM GROOT?
LET'S HOPE SHE LANDED ON SARAWAT, GROOT.
SARAWAT.
THERE'S THE MILANO! AND IT'S TRASHED!
GAMORA?
ARE YOU HERE?
OH, NO.
NOT ONLY IS GAMORA GONE, BUT SO IS QUILL'S CRYPTO-CUBE...
...AND HER SPACE POD!
WHAT? BUT THAT MEANS--
GAMORA GOT OUT BEFORE THE CRASH.
BUT SHE COULD BE HURT...OR WORSE.
LUCKILY, THERE'S A TRACKER ON ALL THE PODS.
WE'LL STAY HERE AND FIX THE SHIP. QUILL--

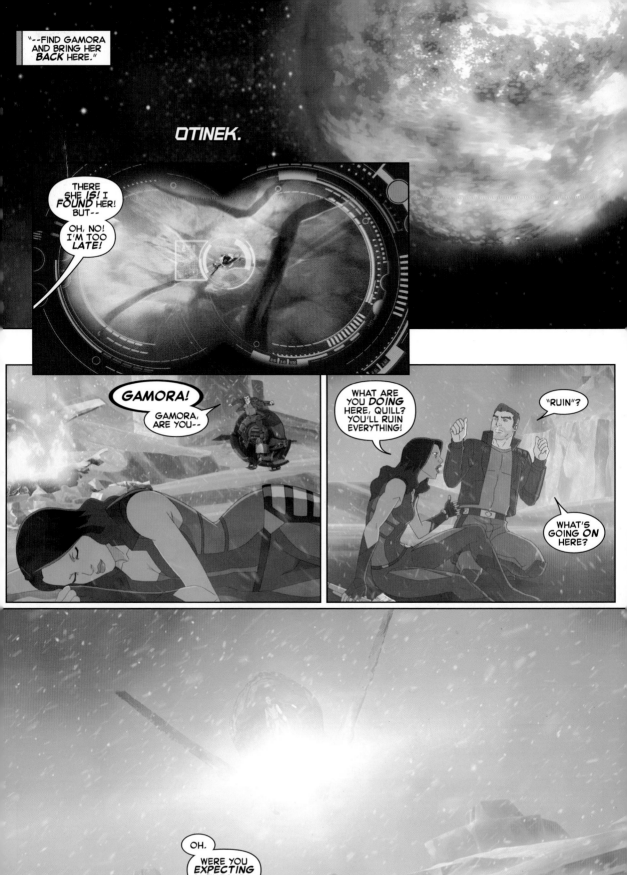

"--FIND GAMORA AND BRING HER *BACK* HERE."

OTINEK.

THERE SHE *IS!* I *FOUND* HER! BUT--

OH, NO! I'M TOO *LATE!*

GAMORA!

GAMORA, ARE YOU--

WHAT ARE YOU *DOING* HERE, QUILL? YOU'LL RUIN EVERYTHING!

"RUIN"?

WHAT'S GOING *ON* HERE?

OH.

WERE YOU *EXPECTING* SOMEONE?

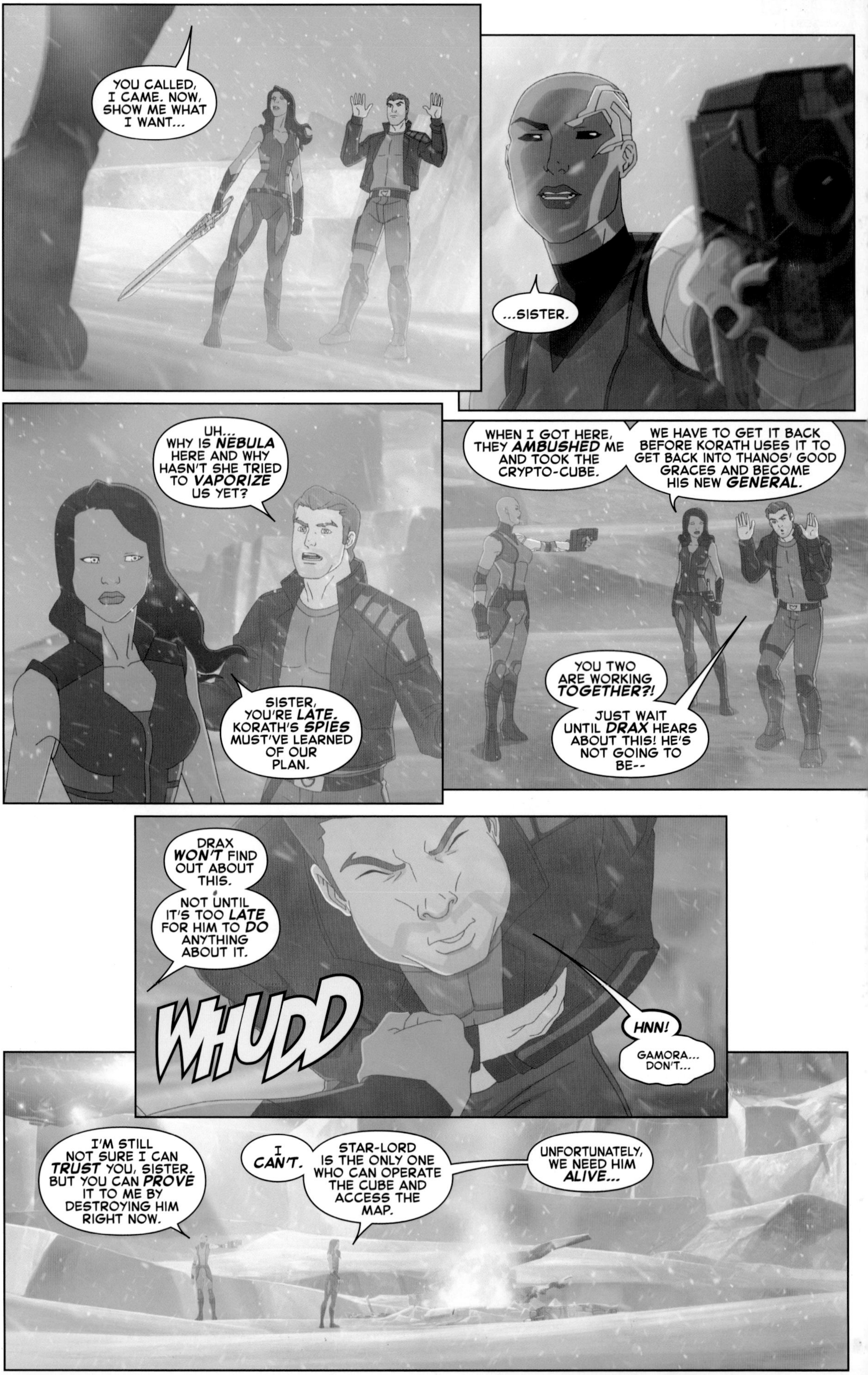

YOU CALLED, I CAME. NOW, SHOW ME WHAT I WANT...
...SISTER.
UH... WHY IS NEBULA HERE AND WHY HASN'T SHE TRIED TO VAPORIZE US YET?
SISTER, YOU'RE LATE. KORATH'S SPIES MUST'VE LEARNED OF OUR PLAN.
WHEN I GOT HERE, THEY AMBUSHED ME AND TOOK THE CRYPTO-CUBE.
WE HAVE TO GET IT BACK BEFORE KORATH USES IT TO GET BACK INTO THANOS' GOOD GRACES AND BECOME HIS NEW GENERAL.
YOU TWO ARE WORKING TOGETHER?!
JUST WAIT UNTIL DRAX HEARS ABOUT THIS! HE'S NOT GOING TO BE--
DRAX WON'T FIND OUT ABOUT THIS.
NOT UNTIL IT'S TOO LATE FOR HIM TO DO ANYTHING ABOUT IT.
WHUDD
HNN!
GAMORA... DON'T...
I'M STILL NOT SURE I CAN TRUST YOU, SISTER. BUT YOU CAN PROVE IT TO ME BY DESTROYING HIM RIGHT NOW.
I CAN'T.
STAR-LORD IS THE ONLY ONE WHO CAN OPERATE THE CUBE AND ACCESS THE MAP.
UNFORTUNATELY, WE NEED HIM ALIVE...

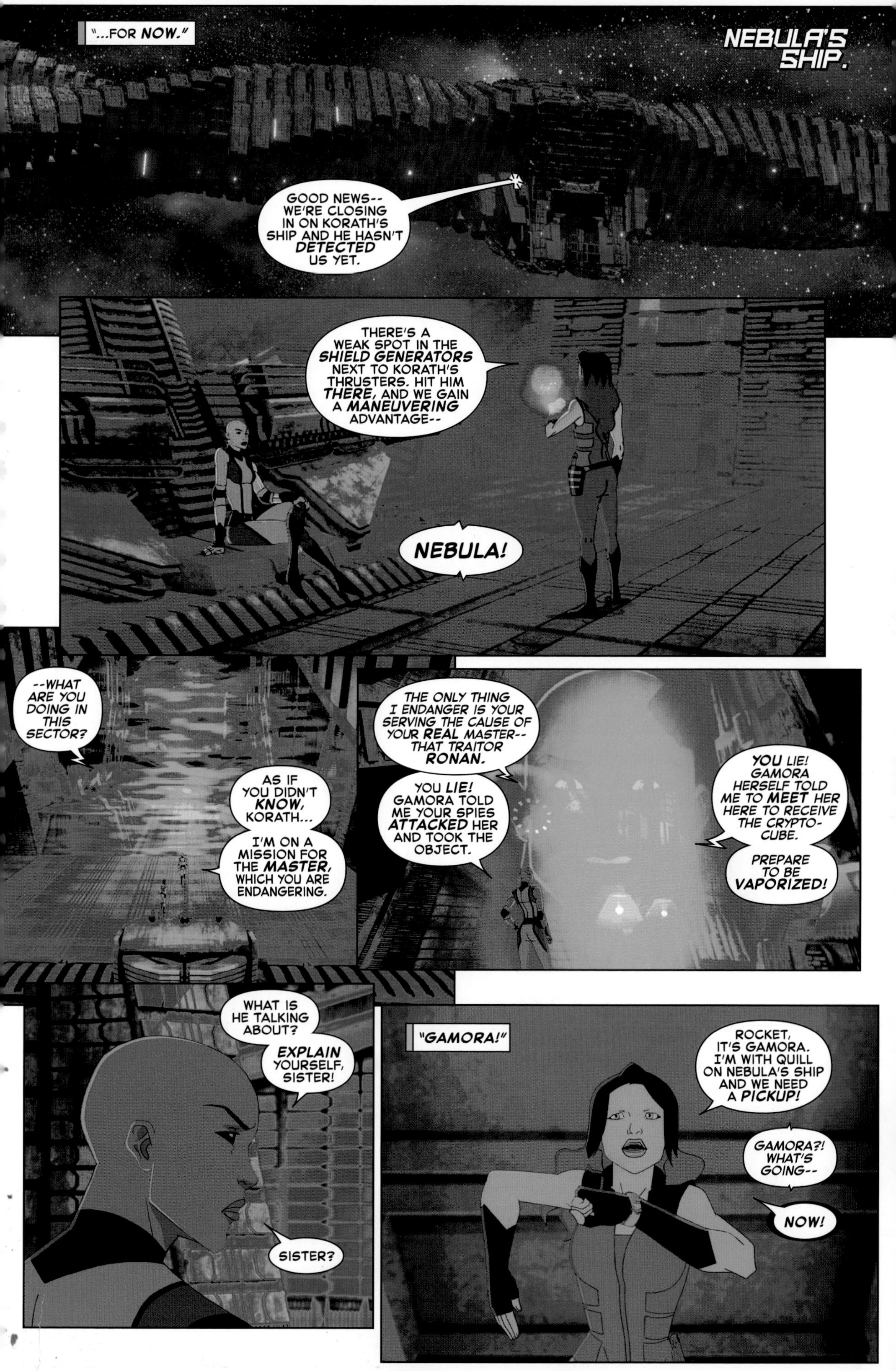
"...FOR NOW."
NEBULA'S SHIP.
GOOD NEWS-- WE'RE CLOSING IN ON KORATH'S SHIP AND HE HASN'T DETECTED US YET.
THERE'S A WEAK SPOT IN THE SHIELD GENERATORS NEXT TO KORATH'S THRUSTERS. HIT HIM THERE, AND WE GAIN A MANEUVERING ADVANTAGE--
NEBULA!
--WHAT ARE YOU DOING IN THIS SECTOR?
AS IF YOU DIDN'T KNOW, KORATH...
I'M ON A MISSION FOR THE MASTER, WHICH YOU ARE ENDANGERING.
THE ONLY THING I ENDANGER IS YOUR SERVING THE CAUSE OF YOUR REAL MASTER-- THAT TRAITOR RONAN.
YOU LIE! GAMORA TOLD ME YOUR SPIES ATTACKED HER AND TOOK THE OBJECT.
YOU LIE! GAMORA HERSELF TOLD ME TO MEET HER HERE TO RECEIVE THE CRYPTO-CUBE.
PREPARE TO BE VAPORIZED!
WHAT IS HE TALKING ABOUT?
EXPLAIN YOURSELF, SISTER!
SISTER?
"GAMORA!"
ROCKET, IT'S GAMORA. I'M WITH QUILL ON NEBULA'S SHIP AND WE NEED A PICKUP!
GAMORA?! WHAT'S GOING--
NOW!

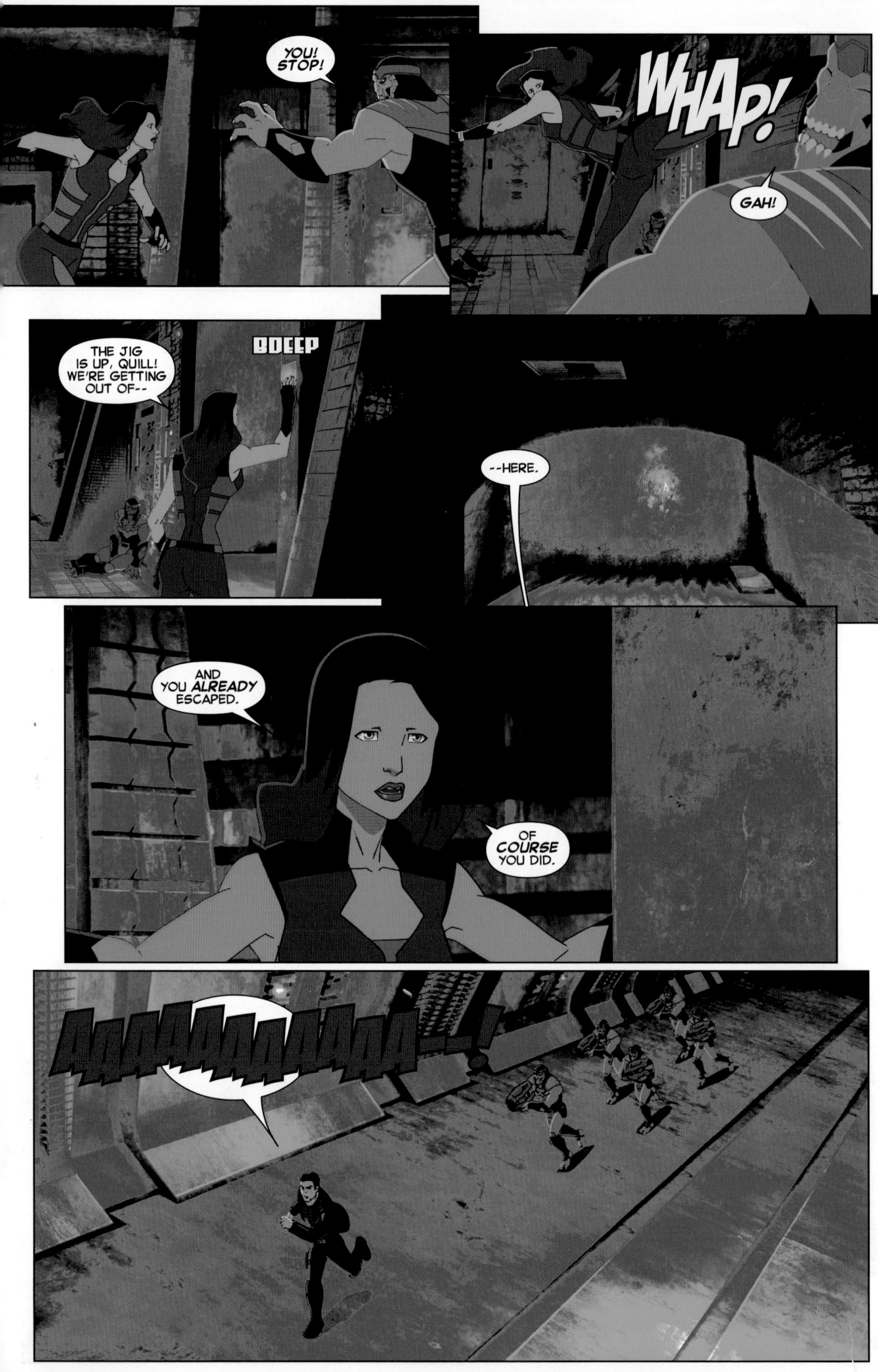
YOU! STOP!
WHAP!
GAH!
THE JIG IS UP, QUILL! WE'RE GETTING OUT OF--
BDEEP
--HERE.
AND YOU ALREADY ESCAPED.
OF COURSE YOU DID.
AAAAAAAAAAAA--!

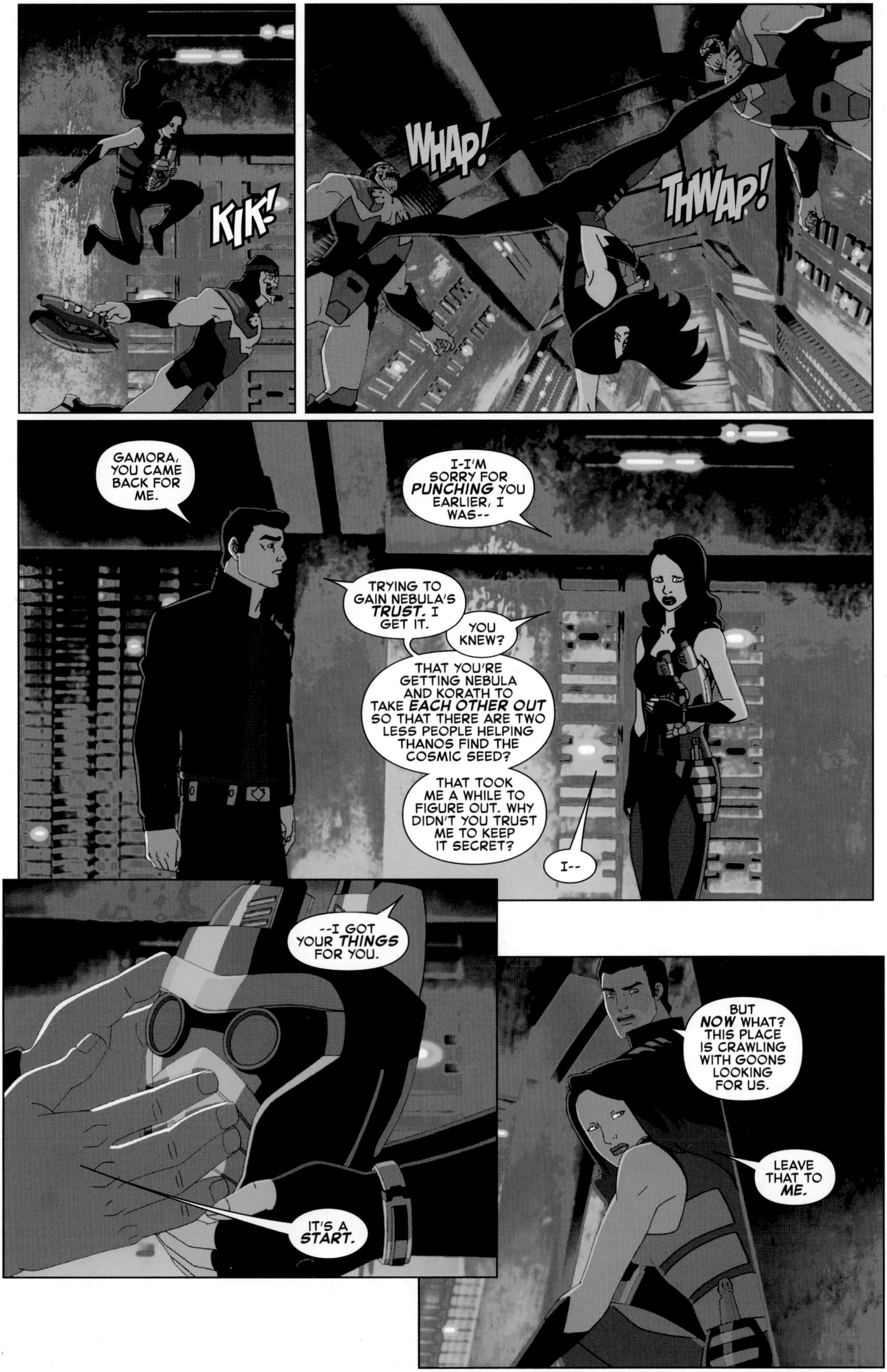
KIK!
WHAP!
THWAP!
GAMORA, YOU CAME BACK FOR ME.
I-I'M SORRY FOR PUNCHING YOU EARLIER, I WAS--
TRYING TO GAIN NEBULA'S TRUST. I GET IT.
YOU KNEW?
THAT YOU'RE GETTING NEBULA AND KORATH TO TAKE EACH OTHER OUT SO THAT THERE ARE TWO LESS PEOPLE HELPING THANOS FIND THE COSMIC SEED?
THAT TOOK ME A WHILE TO FIGURE OUT. WHY DIDN'T YOU TRUST ME TO KEEP IT SECRET?
I--
--I GOT YOUR THINGS FOR YOU.
IT'S A START.
BUT NOW WHAT? THIS PLACE IS CRAWLING WITH GOONS LOOKING FOR US.
LEAVE THAT TO ME.

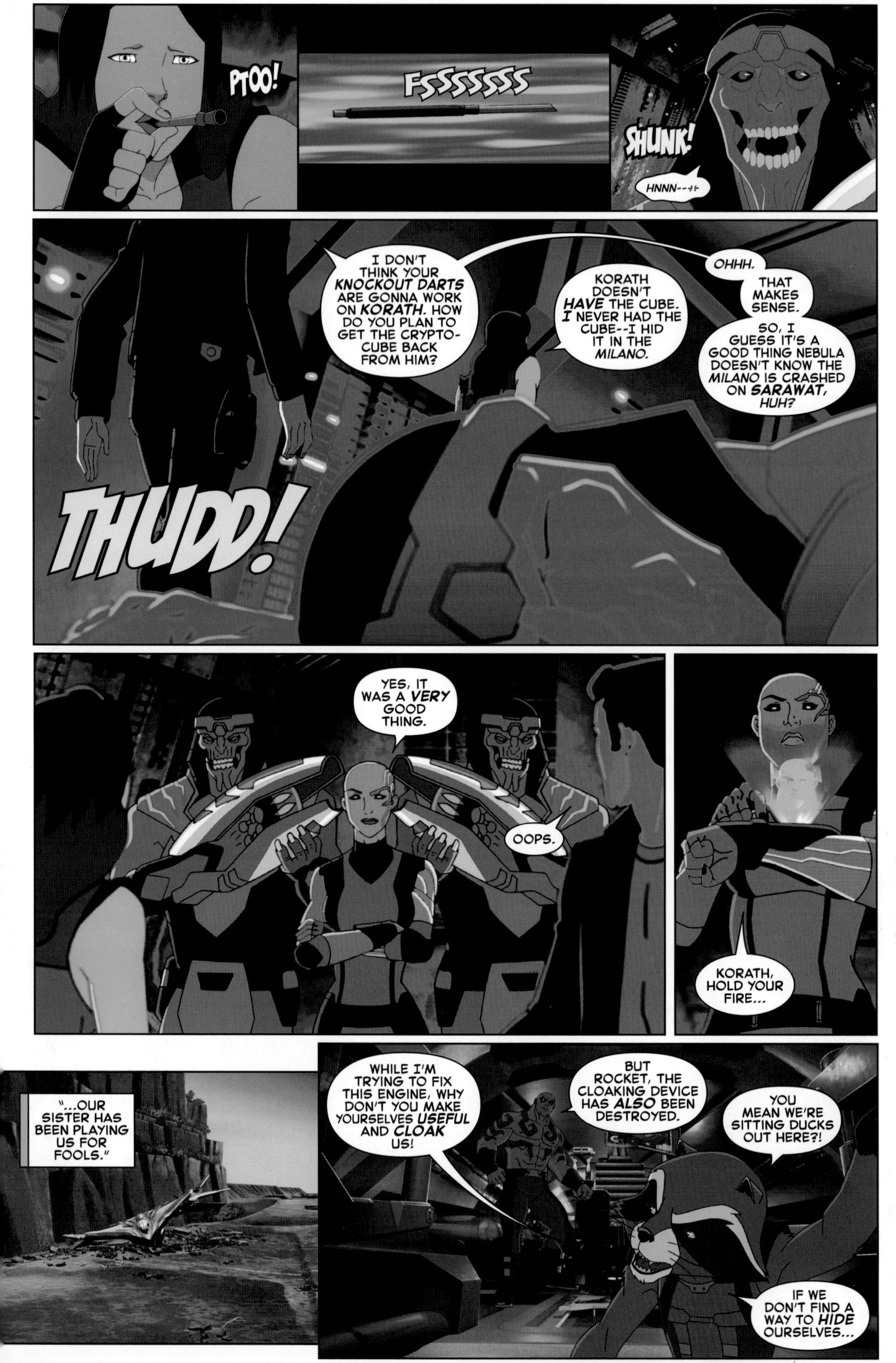
PTOO!
FSSSSSS
SHUNK!
HNNN--‡‡
I DON'T THINK YOUR KNOCKOUT DARTS ARE GONNA WORK ON KORATH. HOW DO YOU PLAN TO GET THE CRYPTO-CUBE BACK FROM HIM?
KORATH DOESN'T HAVE THE CUBE. I NEVER HAD THE CUBE--I HID IT IN THE MILANO.
OHHH.
THAT MAKES SENSE.
SO, I GUESS IT'S A GOOD THING NEBULA DOESN'T KNOW THE MILANO IS CRASHED ON SARAWAT, HUH?
THUDD!
YES, IT WAS A VERY GOOD THING.
OOPS.
KORATH, HOLD YOUR FIRE...
"...OUR SISTER HAS BEEN PLAYING US FOR FOOLS."
WHILE I'M TRYING TO FIX THIS ENGINE, WHY DON'T YOU MAKE YOURSELVES USEFUL AND CLOAK US!
BUT ROCKET, THE CLOAKING DEVICE HAS ALSO BEEN DESTROYED.
YOU MEAN WE'RE SITTING DUCKS OUT HERE?!
IF WE DON'T FIND A WAY TO HIDE OURSELVES...

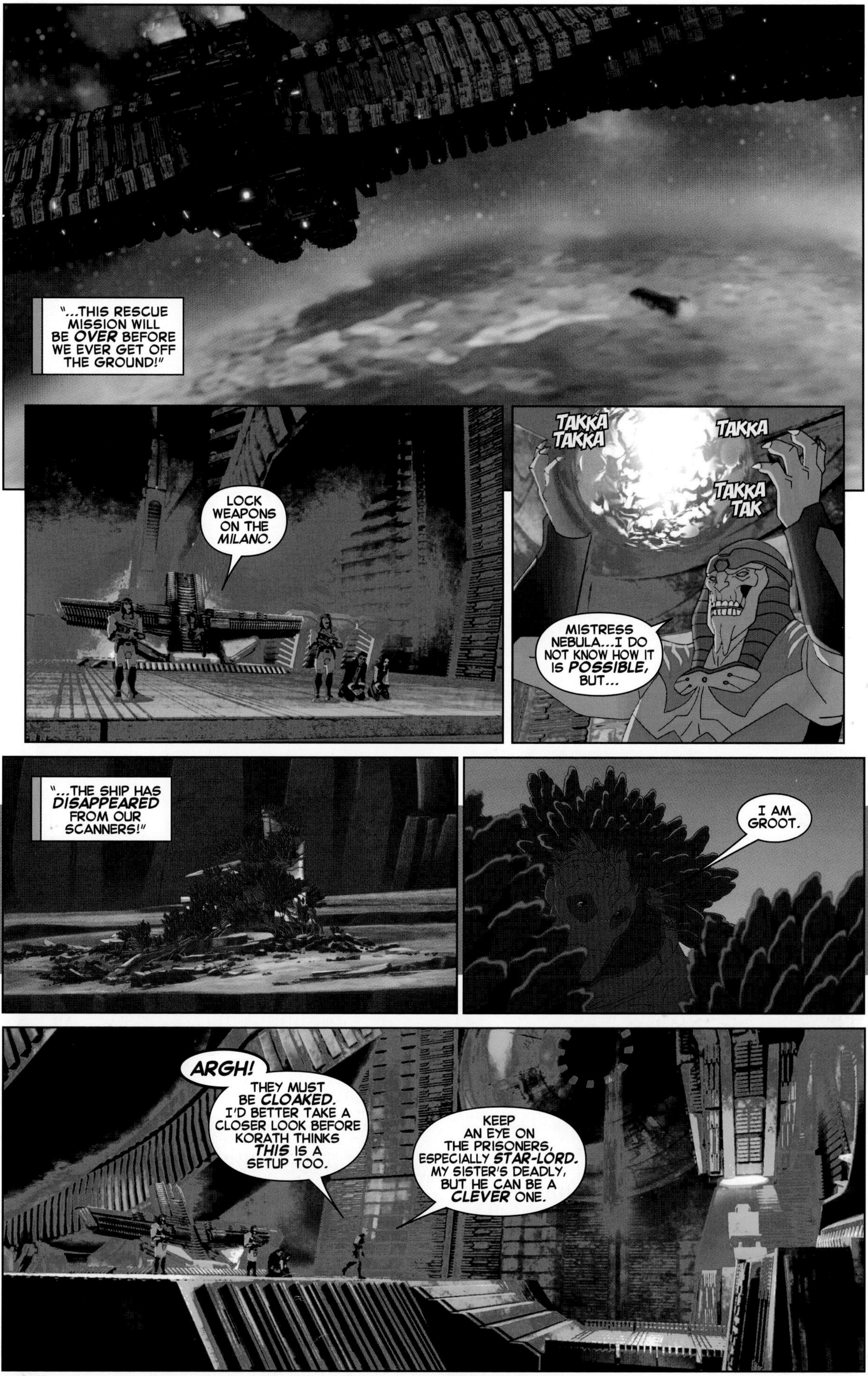
"...THIS RESCUE MISSION WILL BE OVER BEFORE WE EVER GET OFF THE GROUND!"
LOCK WEAPONS ON THE MILANO.
TAKKA TAKKA
TAKKA
TAKKA TAK
MISTRESS NEBULA...I DO NOT KNOW HOW IT IS POSSIBLE, BUT...
"...THE SHIP HAS DISAPPEARED FROM OUR SCANNERS!"
I AM GROOT.
ARGH!
THEY MUST BE CLOAKED. I'D BETTER TAKE A CLOSER LOOK BEFORE KORATH THINKS THIS IS A SETUP TOO.
KEEP AN EYE ON THE PRISONERS, ESPECIALLY STAR-LORD. MY SISTER'S DEADLY, BUT HE CAN BE A CLEVER ONE.

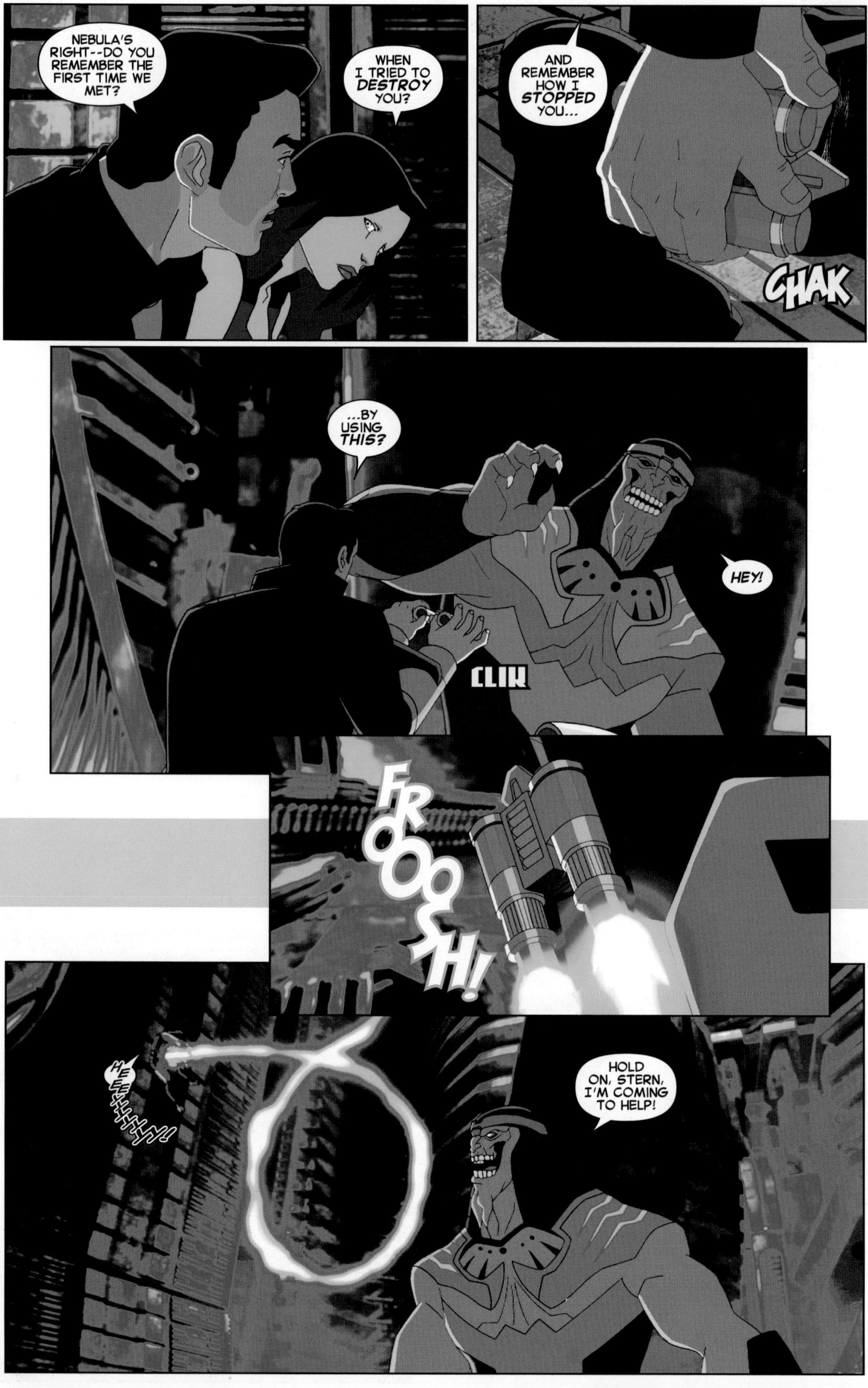
NEBULA'S RIGHT--DO YOU REMEMBER THE FIRST TIME WE MET?
WHEN I TRIED TO DESTROY YOU?
AND REMEMBER HOW I STOPPED YOU...
CHAK
...BY USING THIS?
HEY!
CLIK
FROOOOSH!
HOLD ON, STERN, I'M COMING TO HELP!

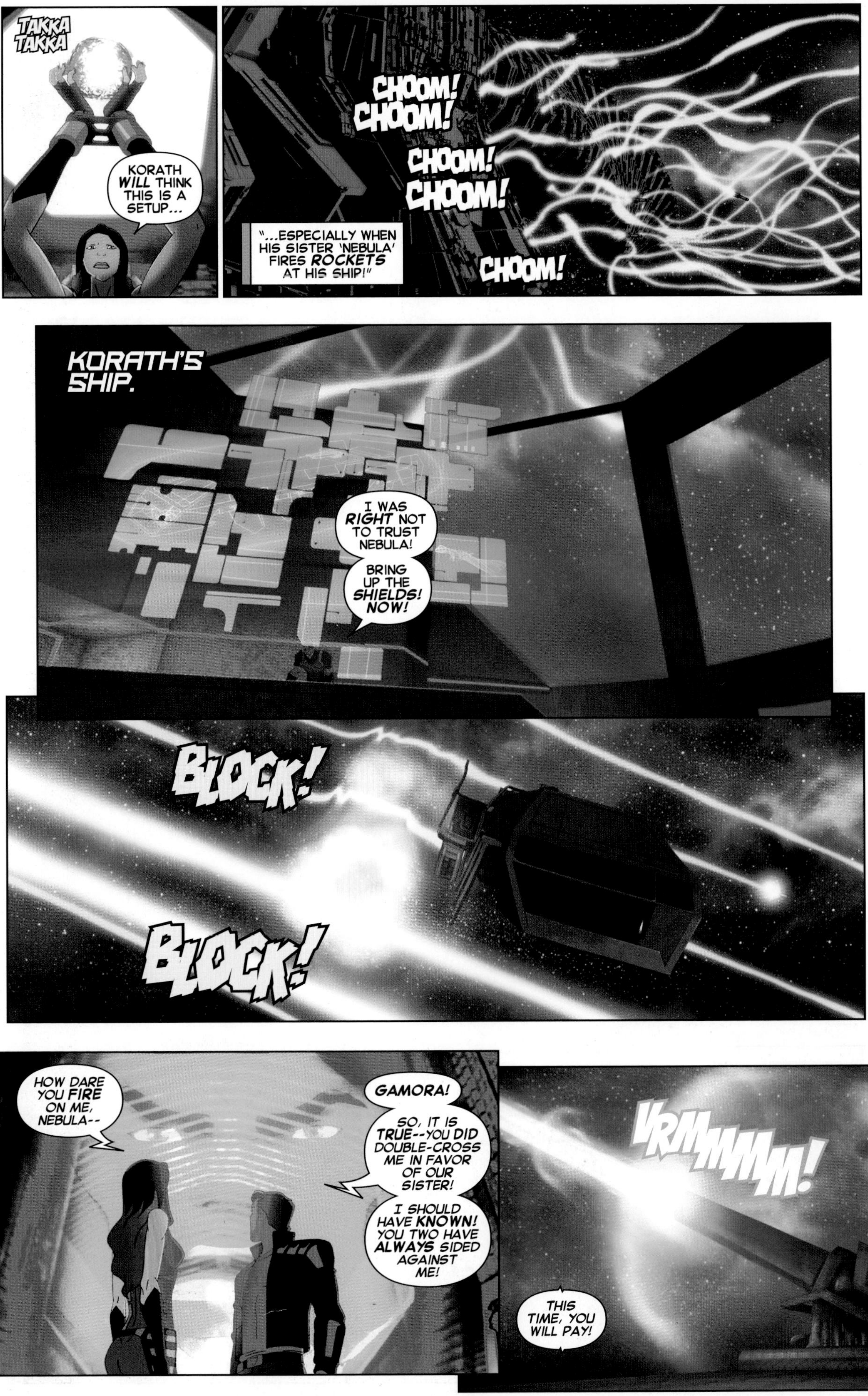
TAKKA TAKKA
KORATH WILL THINK THIS IS A SETUP...
"...ESPECIALLY WHEN HIS SISTER 'NEBULA' FIRES ROCKETS AT HIS SHIP!"
CHOOM! CHOOM!
CHOOM! CHOOM!
CHOOM!
KORATH'S SHIP.
I WAS RIGHT NOT TO TRUST NEBULA!
BRING UP THE SHIELDS! NOW!
BLOCK!
BLOCK!
HOW DARE YOU FIRE ON ME, NEBULA--
GAMORA!
SO, IT IS TRUE--YOU DID DOUBLE-CROSS ME IN FAVOR OF OUR SISTER!
I SHOULD HAVE KNOWN! YOU TWO HAVE ALWAYS SIDED AGAINST ME!
VRMMMMM!
THIS TIME, YOU WILL PAY!

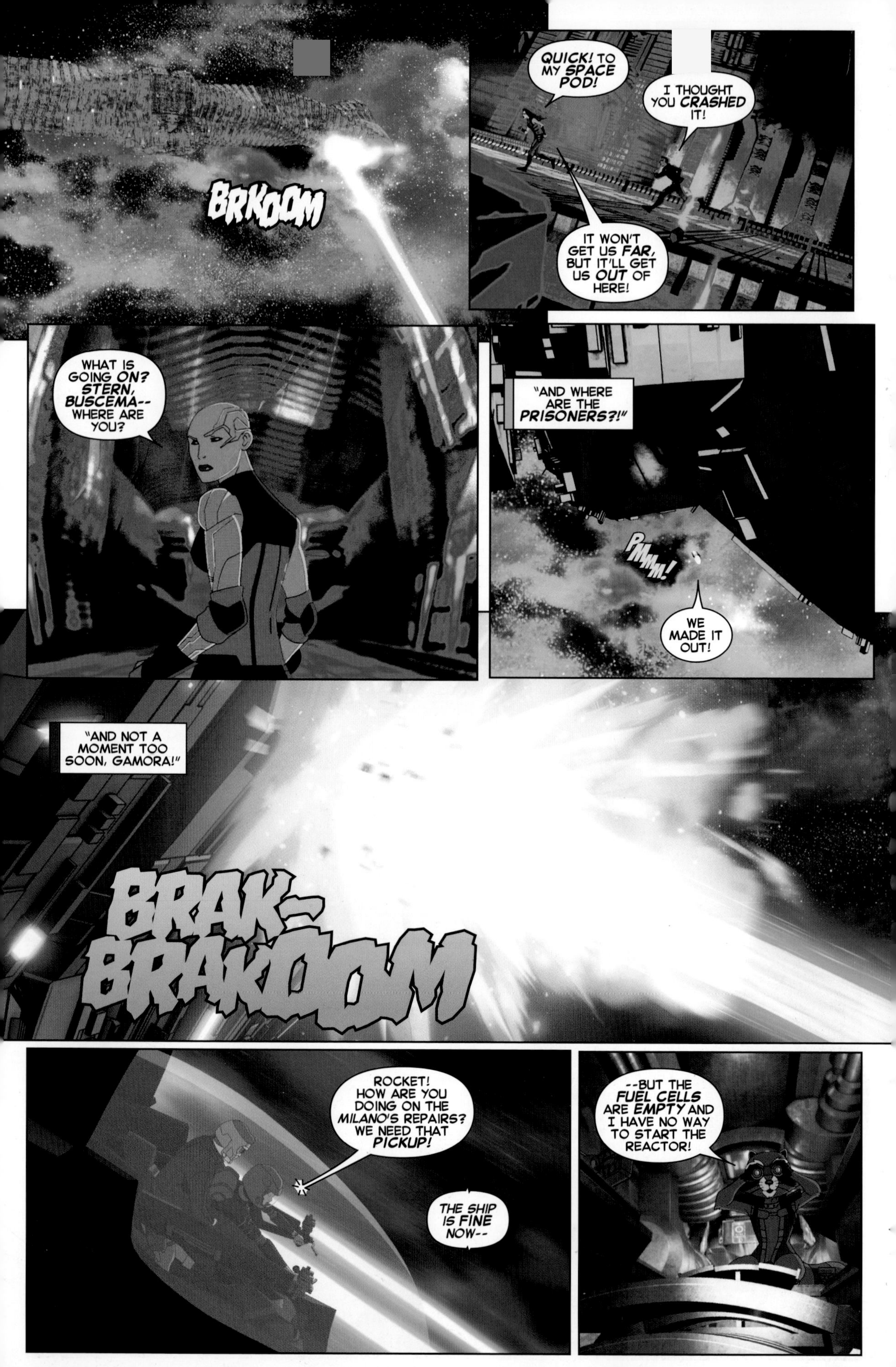
BRKOOM
QUICK! TO MY SPACE POD!
I THOUGHT YOU CRASHED IT!
IT WON'T GET US FAR, BUT IT'LL GET US OUT OF HERE!
WHAT IS GOING ON? STERN, BUSCEMA-- WHERE ARE YOU?
"AND WHERE ARE THE PRISONERS?!"
PMMM!
WE MADE IT OUT!
"AND NOT A MOMENT TOO SOON, GAMORA!"
BRAK-BRAKOOOM
ROCKET! HOW ARE YOU DOING ON THE MILANO'S REPAIRS? WE NEED THAT PICKUP!
THE SHIP IS FINE NOW--
--BUT THE FUEL CELLS ARE EMPTY AND I HAVE NO WAY TO START THE REACTOR!

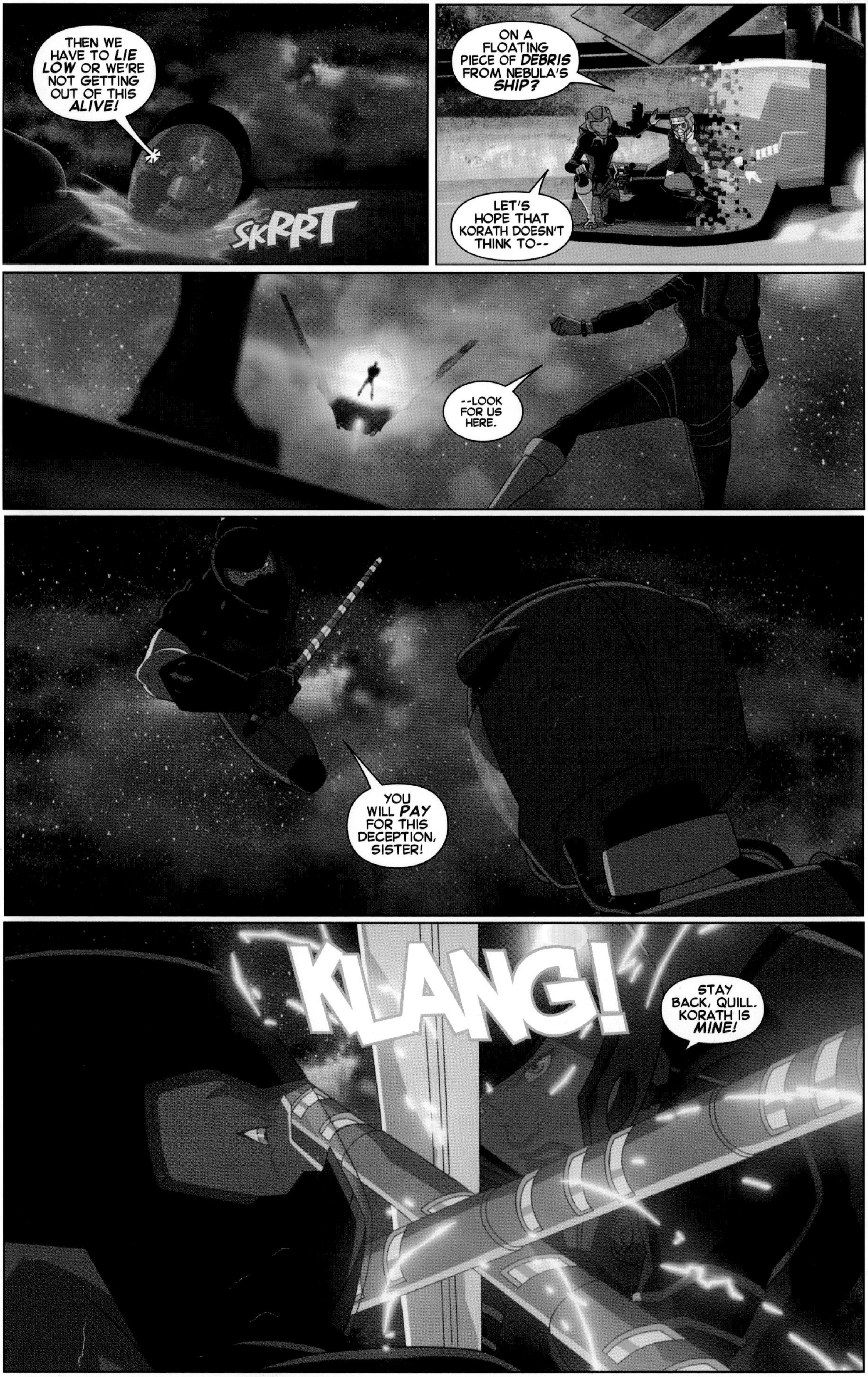
THEN WE HAVE TO LIE LOW OR WE'RE NOT GETTING OUT OF THIS ALIVE!
SKRRT
ON A FLOATING PIECE OF DEBRIS FROM NEBULA'S SHIP?
LET'S HOPE THAT KORATH DOESN'T THINK TO--
--LOOK FOR US HERE.
YOU WILL PAY FOR THIS DECEPTION, SISTER!
KLANG!
STAY BACK, QUILL. KORATH IS MINE!

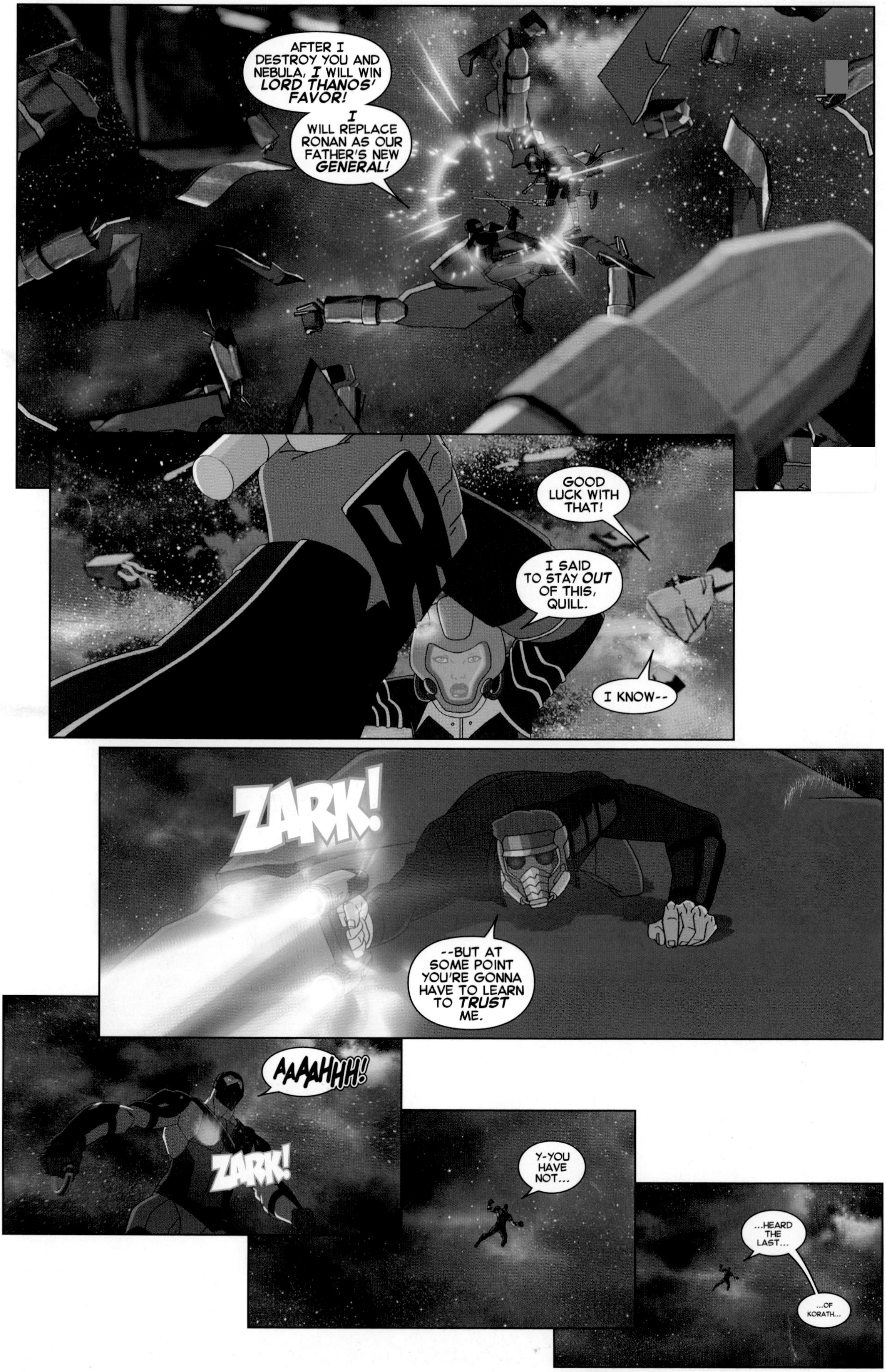
AFTER I DESTROY YOU AND NEBULA, I WILL WIN LORD THANOS' FAVOR!
I WILL REPLACE RONAN AS OUR FATHER'S NEW GENERAL!
GOOD LUCK WITH THAT!
I SAID TO STAY OUT OF THIS, QUILL.
I KNOW--
ZARK!
--BUT AT SOME POINT YOU'RE GONNA HAVE TO LEARN TO TRUST ME.
AAAAHHH!
ZARK!
Y-YOU HAVE NOT...
...HEARD THE LAST...
...OF KORATH...

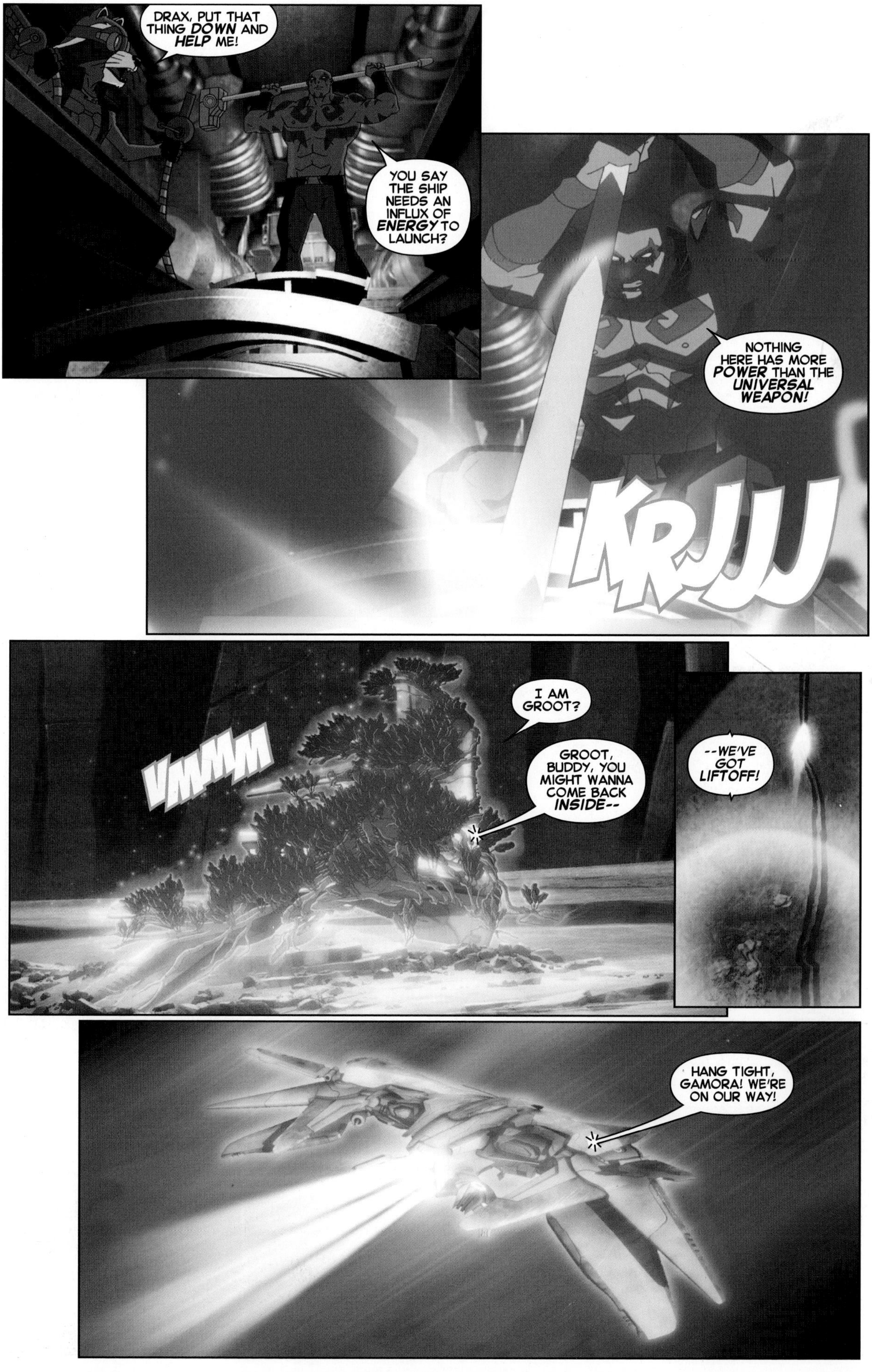
DRAX, PUT THAT THING DOWN AND HELP ME!
YOU SAY THE SHIP NEEDS AN INFLUX OF ENERGY TO LAUNCH?
NOTHING HERE HAS MORE POWER THAN THE UNIVERSAL WEAPON!
KRJJJ
VMMM
I AM GROOT?
GROOT, BUDDY, YOU MIGHT WANNA COME BACK INSIDE--
--WE'VE GOT LIFTOFF!
HANG TIGHT, GAMORA! WE'RE ON OUR WAY!

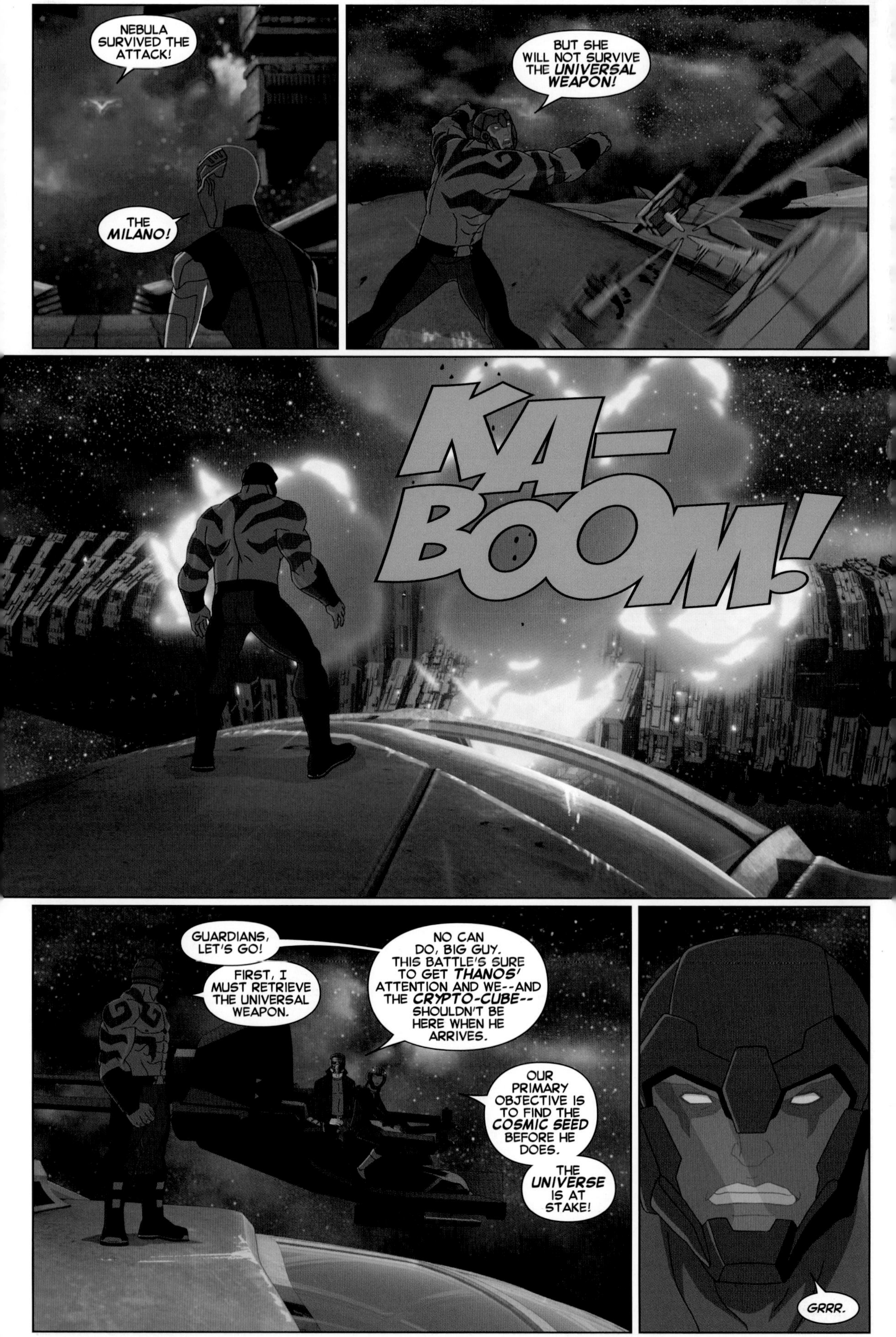
NEBULA SURVIVED THE ATTACK!
THE MILANO!
BUT SHE WILL NOT SURVIVE THE UNIVERSAL WEAPON!
KA-BOOM!
GUARDIANS, LET'S GO!
FIRST, I MUST RETRIEVE THE UNIVERSAL WEAPON.
NO CAN DO, BIG GUY. THIS BATTLE'S SURE TO GET THANOS' ATTENTION AND WE--AND THE CRYPTO-CUBE--SHOULDN'T BE HERE WHEN HE ARRIVES.
OUR PRIMARY OBJECTIVE IS TO FIND THE COSMIC SEED BEFORE HE DOES.
THE UNIVERSE IS AT STAKE!
GRRR.

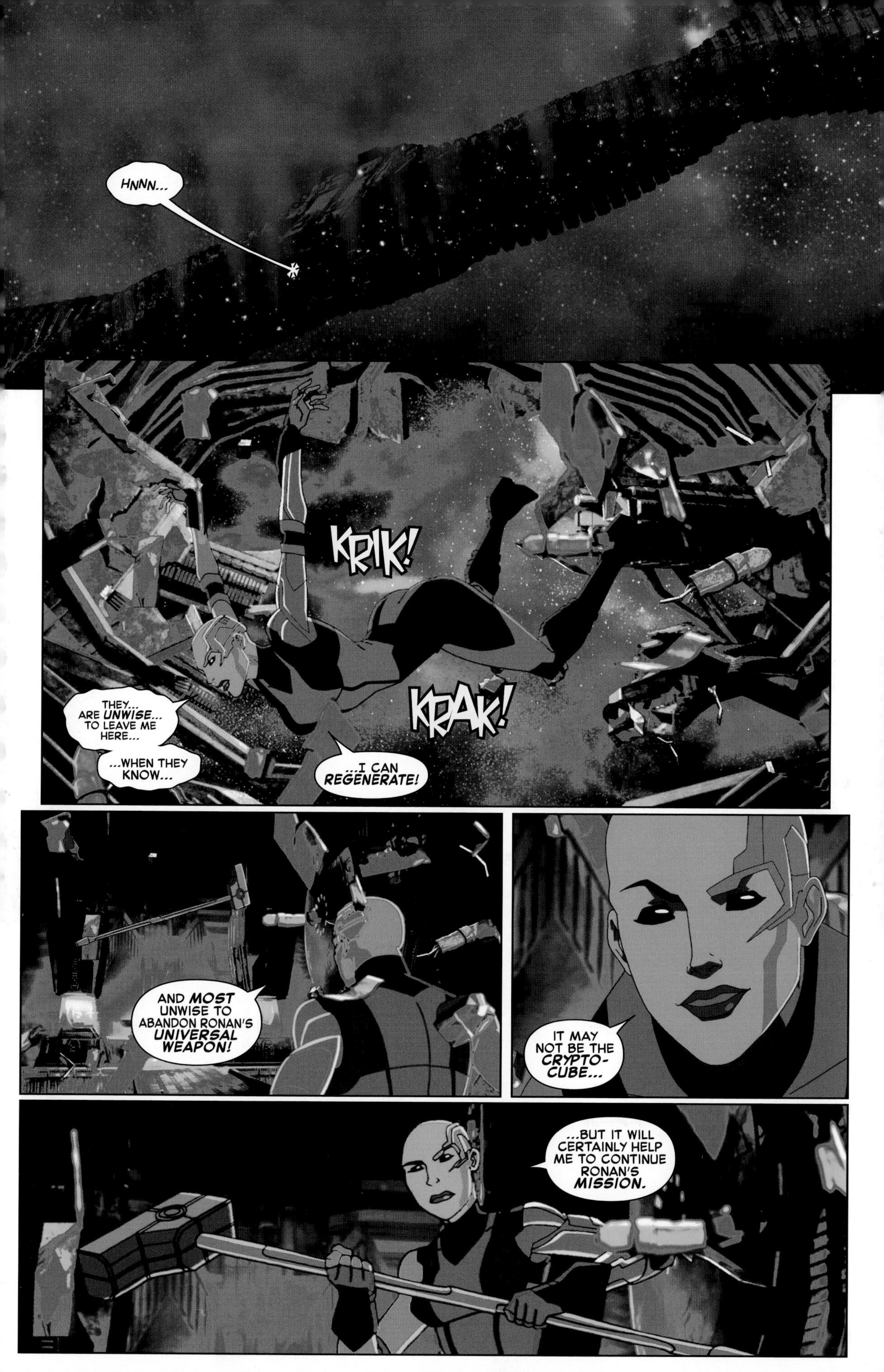

HNNN...
KRIK!
KRAK!
THEY... ARE UNWISE... TO LEAVE ME HERE...
...WHEN THEY KNOW...
...I CAN REGENERATE!
AND MOST UNWISE TO ABANDON RONAN'S UNIVERSAL WEAPON!
IT MAY NOT BE THE CRYPTO-CUBE...
...BUT IT WILL CERTAINLY HELP ME TO CONTINUE RONAN'S MISSION.

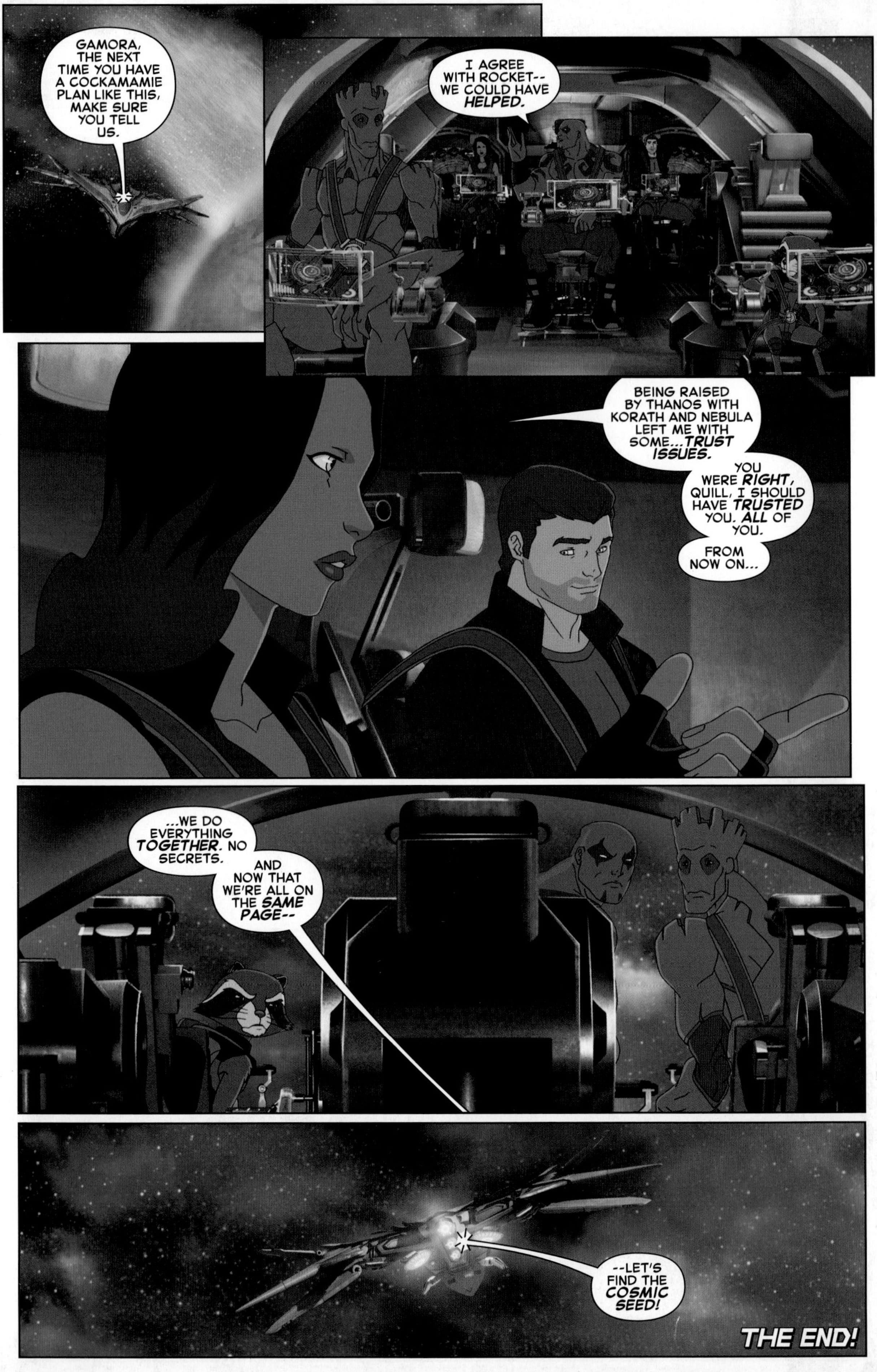
GAMORA, THE NEXT TIME YOU HAVE A COCKAMAMIE PLAN LIKE THIS, MAKE SURE YOU TELL US.
I AGREE WITH ROCKET-- WE COULD HAVE HELPED.
BEING RAISED BY THANOS WITH KORATH AND NEBULA LEFT ME WITH SOME...TRUST ISSUES.
YOU WERE RIGHT, QUILL, I SHOULD HAVE TRUSTED YOU. ALL OF YOU.
FROM NOW ON...
...WE DO EVERYTHING TOGETHER. NO SECRETS.
AND NOW THAT WE'RE ALL ON THE SAME PAGE--
--LET'S FIND THE COSMIC SEED!
THE END!

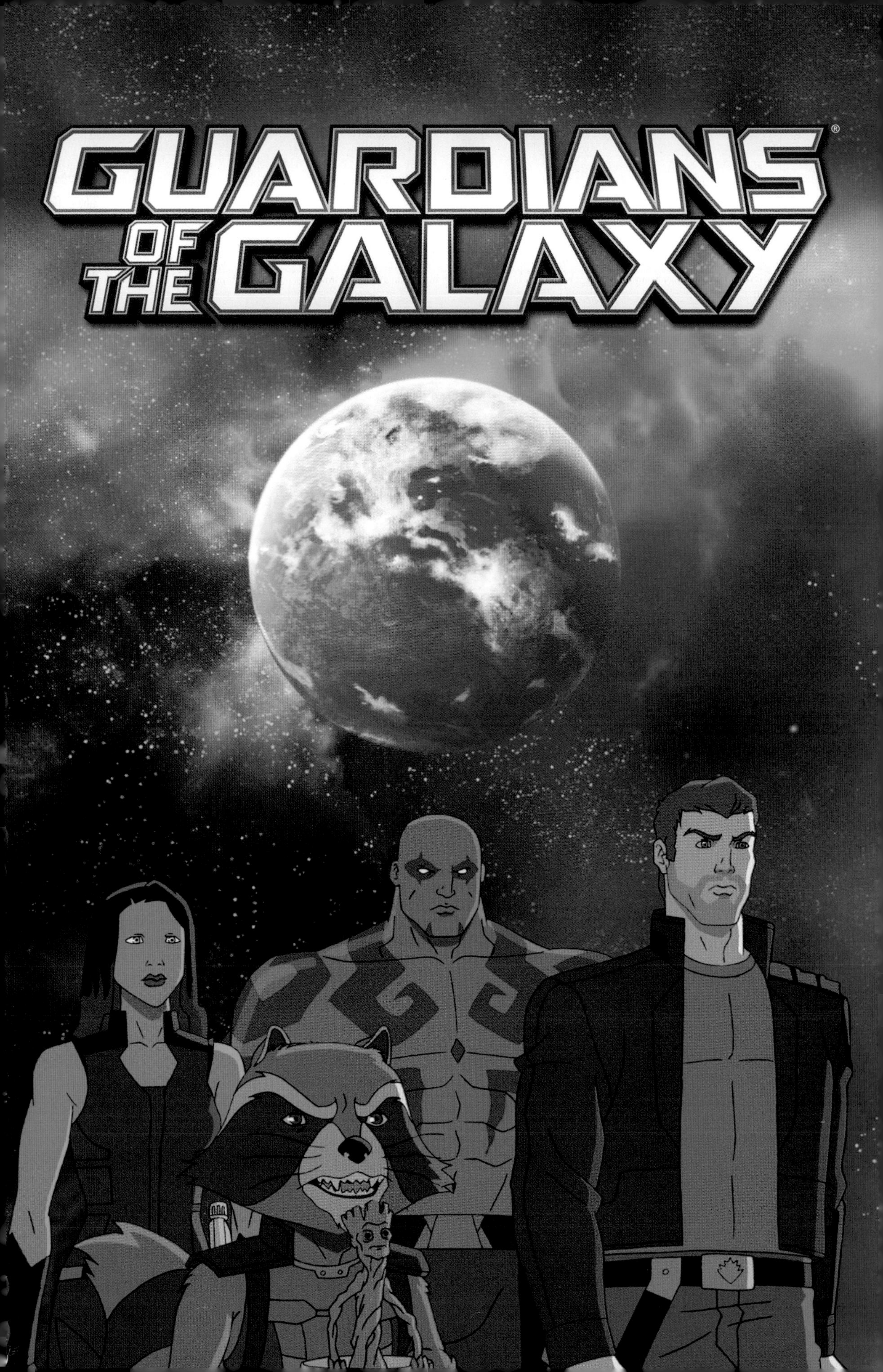
GUARDIANS®
OF THE GALAXY

GUARDIANS OF THE GALAXY

COLLECT THEM ALL!

Set of 6 Hardcover Books ISBN: 978-1-5321-4357-1

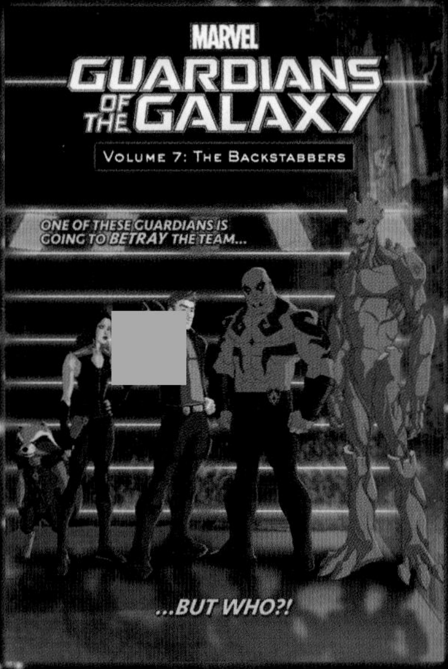
MARVEL
GUARDIANS OF THE GALAXY
VOLUME 7: THE BACKSTABBERS
ONE OF THESE GUARDIANS IS GOING TO BETRAY THE TEAM...
...BUT WHO?!

Hardcover Book ISBN 978-1-5321-4358-8

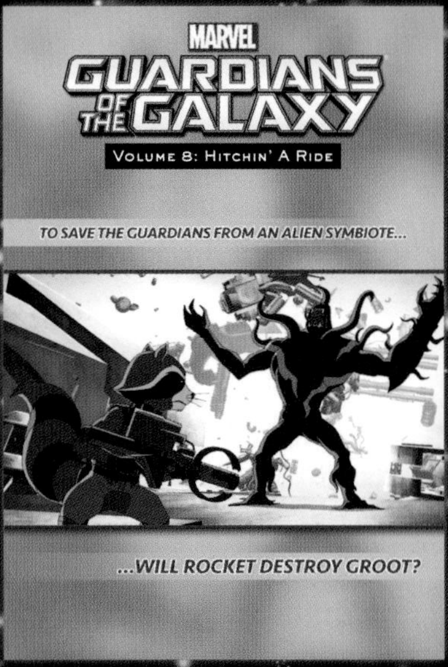
MARVEL
GUARDIANS OF THE GALAXY
VOLUME 8: HITCHIN' A RIDE
TO SAVE THE GUARDIANS FROM AN ALIEN SYMBIOTE...
...WILL ROCKET DESTROY GROOT?

Hardcover Book ISBN 978-1-5321-4359-5

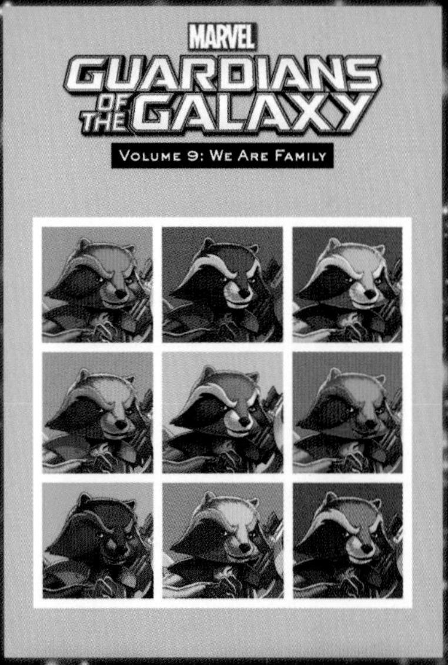
MARVEL
GUARDIANS OF THE GALAXY
VOLUME 9: WE ARE FAMILY

Hardcover Book ISBN 978-1-5321-4360-1

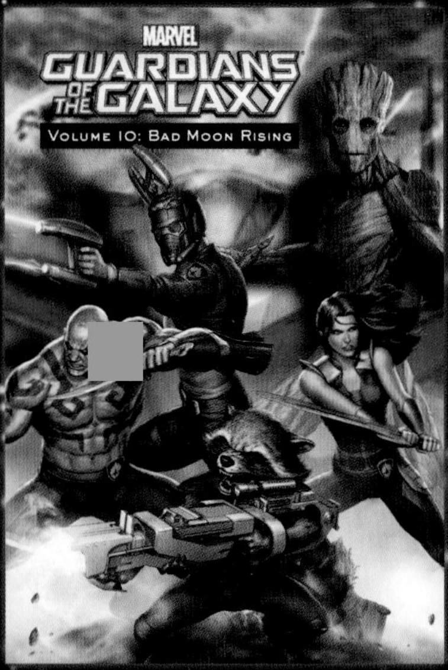
MARVEL
GUARDIANS OF THE GALAXY
VOLUME 10: BAD MOON RISING

Hardcover Book ISBN 978-1-5321-4361-8

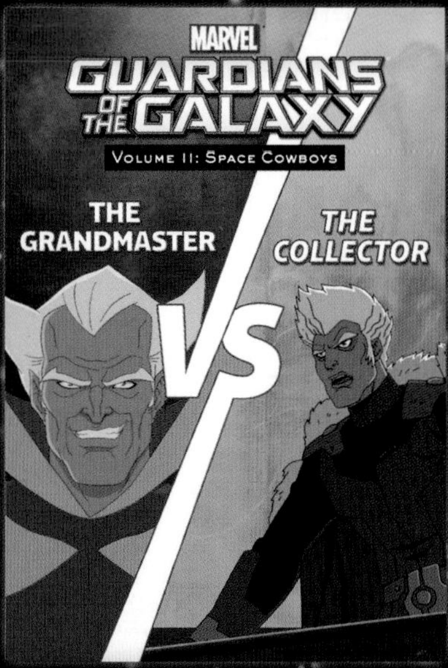
MARVEL
GUARDIANS OF THE GALAXY
VOLUME 11: SPACE COWBOYS
THE GRANDMASTER
VS
THE COLLECTOR

Hardcover Book ISBN 978-1-5321-4362-5

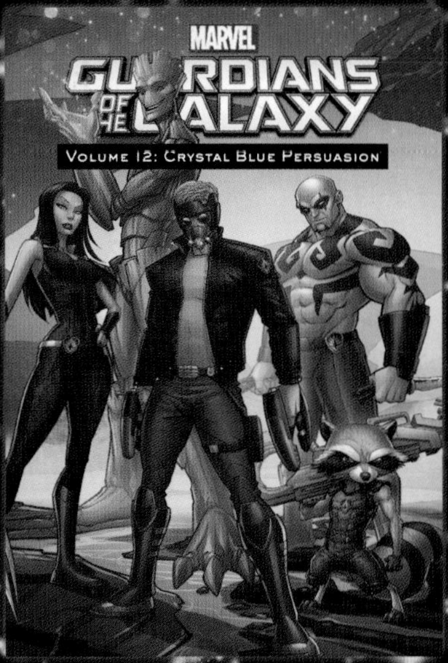
MARVEL
VOLUME 12: CRYSTAL BLUE PERSUASION

Hardcover Book ISBN 978-1-5321-4363-2